THE SPOTLIGHT IS ON YOU!

You are Jem—the hottest rock star around! You and your group, the Holograms, shot to the top of the rock charts and that's just where you have stayed—on top! But as famous as you are, almost no one knows your secret. You are really Jerrica Benton, president of Starlight Music. The Jemstar earrings you always wear are actually mini-transmitters that connect to a super-advanced computer called Synergy. It is Synergy that creates the holographic images that transform you into the totally outrageous Jem.

As Jem, you will lead the glamorous life. Just read the story and follow the directions at the bottom of each page. Hurry up. Get started. It's showtime!

FIND YOUR FATE™®

#2

The Video Caper

by Jean Waricha

BALLANTINE BOOKS • NEW YORK

Library of Congress Catalog Card Number: 86-90789

ISBN: 0-345-33794-8

Editorial services provided by Parachute Press, Inc.

Text design by Gene Siegel

Manufactured in the United States of America

First Edition: December 1986

10 9 8 7 6 5 4 3 2 1

To my mother,
Helen, and to the memory
of my father, John.

Jem™

The Video Caper

"Jerrica! Jerrica!" Rio comes rushing into your office calling your name.

"Yes, Rio," you say, looking up at your favorite guy. "What is it?"

"We're going to London," he tells you, "to shoot the video for Jem's new album *Crown Jewels*. I just made the deal."

"That's wonderful! When do you and Jem leave?" you ask.

"No, you don't get it," Rio replies. "We're all going—you, me, and Jem. After we shoot the video, we can sightsee! We leave tonight."

"Think fast," you tell yourself. "How on earth are you going to get yourself out of *this* situation? There is no way that all three of you can go to London together. You're Jem *and* you're Jerrica!"

"Oh, dear," you tell Rio. "Please don't be upset with me, but I can't leave. I'm swamped with paper work. You and Jem leave tonight and I'll follow you in a few days."

"Well, all right," he says reluctantly. "But promise me that we can spend some time alone in London."

"I promise," you say, giving him a quick kiss on the cheek.

"By the way," says Rio, "where's Jem? I can't wait to tell her."

"She and the Holograms are rehearsing in the studio," you answer.

Before you can stop him, Rio is out the door.

. . . .
Turn to page 2.

1

You've got to get to the rehearsal studio before Rio. You'd better act fast! You touch your Jemstar earrings and instantly transform yourself into Jem. Your white business suit turns into a hot pink minidress. You add a few touches to your makeup, fluff out your pink hair, and you're ready. Before you leave, you can't help but notice yourself in the mirror and think how truly outrageous you look.

You slip through a private door that goes from your office to the recording studio. Shana, Aja, and Kimber are already tuning their musical instruments.

"Lookin' good," Shana tells you, as you step up to the microphone. You glance over at Aja, Kimber, and Shana. "Let's rock 'n' roll!" you say. At once, everything comes together—the music, the lyrics, the voices.

You see Rio enter the studio. He waits until you finish—then walks toward you. "Pack your bags!" he tells you. "We're off to London to make a video of *Crown Jewels*."

"That's wonderful," you say, acting surprised.

"By the way," he adds, "your friend, the Countess du Voisin, will be there, and I've been able to get a real Princess to play a part."

. . . .

Go to page 3.

2

You arrive in London the next morning, check into your hotel, and then go directly to the studio. The set is fantastic! You and the Holograms try on your costumes.

You're happy to see your old friend, the Countess du Voisin, on the set when you arrive. "Countess," you say, "it's so wonderful to see you again."

You'd love to spend time chatting with her, but you see Rio approaching. With him is a beautiful young woman. "Countess, Jem," Rio says formally, "allow me to introduce you to the Princess Sarah Anne Paiget-Smith."

What should you do? Do you curtsey? How do you address a princess? Before you can say anything, the Princess steps forward.

"Please call me Sarah," she tells you. "You can't imagine what a thrill it is to meet someone as famous as you."

Sarah isn't stuck-up at all. In a matter of moments, you know that the two of you are going to be great friends.

"Jem," says the Countess, "why don't you, the Holograms, and Princess Sarah come to my home this afternoon for tea. You can take my car. It's parked downstairs."

Turn to page 4.

"What a wonderful idea!" you say. "Do we have time, Rio?"

"Yes," he answers, "but take the rehearsal tape with you. Maybe you can play it in the car on the way down."

"Okay," you agree, taking the tape and slipping it into your pocket. All Rio seems to think about these days is work and Jem. If he only knew. . . .

. . . .

Turn to page 54.

It's Rio!

"Oh, Rio," you shout. "You sure gave us a scare, but I'm still glad to see you. How did you find us?" you ask, giving him a friendly hug—after all, he's Jerrica's boyfriend, not Jem's.

"Shana told me," he says, "and I just followed the same tire tracks you did. But now that I'm here, you girls should go home."

"No way, Rio," you say. "We've . . . Rio, I feel . . . strange . . . faint . . . Ohh!!" A hissing sound fills the cabin.

"Knock-out gas," he shouts. "Hold your breath. I'm going to try to block the gas."

Rio takes off his jacket and tries to stuff it into the vent above you.

"It's a trap!" he says. "Someone must have been in here all along!"

You hear the engines starting up. The plane is taking off.

"Too . . . late, . . ." you say, sliding to the floor. You're out cold.

. . . .

Turn to page 26.

Eric comes closer to you.

"I know Jerrica Benton's father was some kind of computer genius. Before he died, he built a type of super computer that can transform energy. I know you have that machine and I know it has something to do with your success."

Eric leans forward. His face turns red with anger.

"I want that computer!! And I want to know the secret way you and Jerrica control it." His shouts echo through the room.

"But, Eric, . . ." you start to say.

He continues to shout, "You've escaped from me before, Jem, but not this time. This time I took out a little insurance policy." He stands behind Sarah's chair to make sure you get the point.

"Eric," you try to reason with him, "I don't know what you're talking about. Jerrica is my boss, that's all. I don't know anything about a super computer."

You've got to stall for time. Eric is losing control. There's no way of telling what he might do! What are *you* going to do?

If you think you should stall and try to bluff Eric, turn to page 38.

If you think you should try to make a break for it now, before it's too late, turn to page 25.

6

"Aja," you whisper, "the Princess could be in this room, too. We've got to look in here first."

"Okay," says Aja. "But let's hurry."

You put out your candles and enter the darkened room. Suddenly, a hand grabs you and pulls you forward. You stumble into the room and Aja follows. You barely make out the shape of a person moving toward you. Then the figure lights a candle, and you can see it's an old woman. She walks toward you.

"Why, you're Jem," she says sweetly in an American accent. "And you're Aja, one of the Holograms. I just love your music. Don't be afraid of me."

It seems odd that a woman of her age would be a Jem fan, but not impossible. You take a good look at the woman. Her gray hair is in a bun and she's wearing old-fashioned clothes. You decide she has a kind face.

"Who are you?" you ask.

"I'm Ethel Raymond," she answers. "I'm Eric Raymond's grandmother."

Turn to page 45.

Eric smiles at you. He glances around and spots Aja and Kimber at the buffet table. "I see your whole entourage is with you," Eric says.

Rio steps forward, but you stop him. Zipper, a thug who works for Raymond, is lurking in the background, waiting for a chance to throw a punch at Rio.

"So you figured out my little game. I must remember never to underestimate you, Jem. You're not as dumb as you look," Eric says, insultingly.

You glance over at Rio and see that he's about to slug Eric. Although you would love to see Raymond get it right here and now, there are still many questions to be answered.

Quick! Rio practically has smoke coming out of his ears! What are you going to do?

. . . .

Let Rio deal with Eric? Turn to page 63.

Try to keep him and your temper under control? Turn to page 24.

8

"I'll follow the Misfits," you tell yourself, "and find out where they're going and what they're doing in London."

You walk to the elevator.

"Sorry, Miss Jem," says the security guard, "the lift is on the way down. It'll be just a few minutes until it returns."

"Oh, well," you say, casually, "where's the staircase? I can just as easily walk down. No problem."

"Twenty-four floors?" he asks, showing you the door to the stairs.

You start down the stairs. You quickly bounce down the first five flights. The second five slow you a little. After the next five, you are a little breathless and your legs are shaky. After another three flights, you look at your watch and realize that Pizzazz and Stormer must be long gone by now. You'll never catch them.

. . . .

You might as well go back upstairs and meet the Princess. Start climbing and turn to page 61.

The plane sinks lower.

"It's sand!" shouts Rio. You open your eyes as he neatly lands the plane. Everyone is safe! But what about Sarah, is she safe? And how are you going to get out of here?

Somehow you know these are important questions, but right now, just being alive is a gift.

"Hey," you say, tapping Rio on the arm, "want to go for a dip?" That sounds like a good idea. Cool off now, then you'll be ready for more adventure the next time you dip into THE VIDEO CAPER.

THE END

"All right," you tell Aja, "we'll try the tower first. Here, you go first. I'll follow."

Slowly you walk up the stairs. The flights are steep, but you keep climbing. If Sarah is up there, you've got to save her! When you finally reach the top, you see a long narrow corridor ahead of you. The walls are made of stone and you have the awful feeling that you're in a tomb.

"There's a light on in the room at the end," says Aja. "Can you see it? Look under the doorway."

"Yes," you say. "Let's go!"

As you and Aja walk down the corridor, you notice that the door to one of the rooms is open.

"Look," you whisper to Aja. "That door is open. Maybe we should see what's inside. We might find something we can use to protect ourselves."

"I don't need protection," says Aja doing a quick karate move on an invisible enemy. "Let's go directly to the tower room. We've got to hurry. Zipper might come back any minute now!"

· ·

If you decide to look inside the room closer to you, turn to page 7.

If you decide to go to the tower room, turn to page 33.

11

"Quickly, Aja," you say, "take the old lady and hide behind the curtains."

You blow out the candle and hide behind a chair. The door slowly opens. The light from the corridor illuminates a figure who enters the room.

"Inside, you," says the figure, dragging a second person into the room.

You recognize Zipper. And he has Shana with him! You must do something before Zipper finds you.

You touch your Jemstar earrings. Instantly the floor is covered with snakes. At the same time, you grab Shana and pull her behind your chair.

"Shana," you whisper, "it's me, Jem. Don't be afraid."

"Snakes! Snakes!" shouts Zipper, shining his flashlight on the floor. "Holy cow!"

They may be just holographic images but they're real enough to scare Zipper. He runs out the door screaming.

"Outrageous! Truly outrageous!" Shana says appreciatively.

Suddenly, the old woman makes a break for the door. She's pretty fast for an old lady—in fact, she's getting away.

Turn to page 55.

"Don't touch my hair," cries Pizzazz. "Not after it took me three weeks to get the right shade of green."

"Make it quick, girl," says Shana.

"Okay, the Princess is downstairs. She's tied up in the drawing room off the main hallway. She's just the bait to get you."

"Let her up," you say. "But hold onto her. I've got an idea."

You, Aja, and Shana lead Pizzazz downstairs and enter the drawing room. Sarah is tied to a straight-back chair. You quickly untie her.

"What's going on?" she asks. "Who is that strange-looking woman?"

"I'm sorry about all this, Sarah," you say. "I'll explain later. But first, we've got to leave a little surprise for Eric."

You tie Pizzazz to the chair in Sarah's place.

"Outrageous," says Shana, "you've done it again!"

THE END

13

The plane dips lower and lower. Rio is struggling to keep it aloft. Your eyes skim the countryside. You spot water.

"Rio, there's the water. That means beach . . . sand . . . flat land."

Rio maneuvers the plane toward the water. The jungle grows right to the edge of the water. No luck. Huge rocks appear on the beach. You hold your breath. Your heart is pounding so loud, Rio *must* hear it. You turn away so he won't see how frightened you are, and brace yourself for the crash.

. . . .
Turn to page 10.

You must take a chance, Sarah's safety comes first!

"If you tell us where the Princess is, we'll let that slimy grandson of yours go free. You have my word."

"He has her in the tower room," the old woman whispers. You turn to leave, but she stops you.

"Not that way, they've got armed guards at the door. Come over here," she says, walking to the bookcase. She starts to take books out of the case.

"This old house has many secrets. Behind this bookcase is a passageway that leads directly to the tower room," the old lady tells you.

As she pulls out the last book, a section of the bookcase slides back to reveal a hidden passage.

"Let's go," says Aja, stepping into the darkness.

Should you stop Aja? This could be a trap. Can you really trust any relative of the nasty Eric Raymond?

If you decide to use the passageway, turn to page 70.
If you think it is a trap, turn to page 64.

You, Aja, and Kimber get out of the Countess's car. "Ready for action," you say. "Let's go!" You set a quick pace, jogging beside the tire tracks.

"I know we wanted to see the English countryside," says Kimber, a little breathless, "but this is ridiculous."

"Slow down," says Aja, "I think I see something ahead."

"Right," you say. "It looks like an airfield."

You spot the Mercedes parked next to a small plane. No one seems to be around. A small ticket shack sits on the edge of the field.

"Jem!" cries Aja, "look at the plane. It says *Eric Raymond Enterprises.*"

"I should have known!" you exclaim. Eric Raymond will do *anything* to ruin your career. Ever since your Dad died, Eric has done everything possible to cause you grief. This time he has gone too far.

"Stay here," you tell everyone. "I'm going to get a closer look and see what I can find out."

Turn to page 65.

"No doorway!" cries Aja. "What will we do?"

"It's okay," you assure her. "Here's another hallway and I think I see a door down there." But there's no door at the end of the second hallway—just another hallway. Now, you're frightened. Your heart beats faster. Something is definitely wrong.

"What should we do? Should we go back?" asks Aja.

"No," you answer, trying to stay calm. "This has to end somewhere! We've got to keep going."

The hallway winds around to another, and then another. You're beginning to get dizzy. The candle is growing shorter. Pretty soon, it will go out.

"Here!" you cry, "It's the rope. Pull it."

Aja quickly pulls the rope. Something is happening to the floor. It's crumbling! You're falling!

. . . .

Turn to page 60.

"Aja," you say, "it's Eric Raymond and another one of his thugs. Get ready! I'm going to get Synergy to help us out. You take care of the two men. I'll do as much as I can."

"Ready, Jem," replies Aja, setting herself in a karate stance.

You touch your Jemstar earrings. "Bats, Synergy," you whisper. "Let there be bats."

Turn to page 29.

You touch your earrings. The fireplace instantly comes alive, as huge flames leap from the hearth. They appear to reach right out at Zipper and Eric. It looks like the whole room is in flames. Zipper runs for the door and Eric backs into the farthest corner.

"Jem," says Sarah, "run, save yourself."

"It's okay, Sarah," you say, untying her ropes.

You and Sarah race for the door. You must hurry. In moments Eric and Zipper will be after you.

Turn to page 49.

"We must get to the Countess's estate and notify the authorities," you say.

"I agree," says Kimber. "But first, we've got to fix this tire!"

You, Aja, and Kimber are able to fix the tire without wasting too much time. Aja reads you the map and you drive directly to the Countess's estate. The Countess greets you at the door when you arrive.

"Jem, I was getting worried about you," she says. "Come into the library." Once inside, you tell her what has happened. She listens calmly.

"I knew *something* was wrong," she says, walking toward the desk. "This note came for you just minutes before you arrived." She hands you a sealed note. Your name is typed on the envelope. A chill runs down your spine as you read the note:

> *If you want to see the Princess alive,*
> *go to the old deserted castle in Tannington*
> *Wells. No police. Come alone. Someone will*
> *be watching you.*

Turn to page 31.

"Come in! Come in!"

Now you recognize the voice. It's Zipper, Eric Raymond's stooge. You should have guessed! Eric will stop at nothing to cause trouble for you. He's kidnapped Princess Sarah, but he's probably after you.

Zipper leads you into a large room off the main hallway. The room is empty except for a single lamp, a table, and two chairs. A fire crackles in the fireplace.

Seated in those two chairs are Eric Raymond and Princess Sarah who appears to be tied to the chair.

You smile at Sarah to comfort her, since she appears really frightened. Eric sits behind the table and motions to Zipper to walk over to him.

"You see," Eric says to Zipper, "I told you she would come alone. Little Miss Goody-Two-Shoes. She always does as she's told."

Zipper snickers to himself. Eric stands and faces you. He says, "I've got you right where I want you, my dear. You're going to tell me everything I want to know. And soon."

"What is it you want, Eric?" you say, bravely. "What could I possibly have that you would go to all this trouble to get?"

"It's your secret, Jem. I want your secret!"

Turn to page 6.

21

"Jem," Aja says, "this is a closet. Great going!"

"Okay, okay," you say, and return to your exploration of the main hallway. "It's got to be here somewhere."

Clang. Clang.

"There's that sound again," you say. "Aja, over here. I found the doorway."

This time the door leads down a twisting staircase which ends in the middle of a long underground hallway.

"Now which way?" asks Aja. "Right or left?"

If you decide to go left, turn to page 71.
If you decide to go right, turn to page 59.

Before you can answer, the Misfits charge down the road on motorcycles. They throw smoke bombs and jeer as they ride around you. You just knew they were going to cause trouble!

"Quickly," you shout, "everyone back to the car!"

Somehow everyone reaches the car safely, or so you think.

"Where's Sarah?" you ask, looking around.

Too late! You look out the window just in time to see a big black Mercedes stop. Two men jump out, grab Sarah and get back into their sedan.

"Oh no!" you gasp. "She's being kidnapped!"

Your heart sinks to your knees. What are you going to do? You've got to save her!

Should you drive on to the Countess's estate and notify the authorities? Or will you lose too much time that way?

Maybe you should follow the Mercedes and try to rescue the Princess.

If you decide to drive straight to the Countess's estate, turn to page 20.

If you decide to follow the Mercedes, turn to page 46.

You hold on to Rio's arm. He doesn't move. His fists are tightly clenched, but he stays in control.

You have no idea what Eric is talking about, but it must have something to do with the kidnapping and your mysterious airplane ride.

"What did you hope to accomplish by your little game?" you ask, hoping Eric will explain.

"That's easy. I hired Candy Lane to sabotage your little video," he says, pointing to the so-called princess. "Why, the overtime alone would have run into the millions! Plus, when everyone found out your princess was a fraud, you would have been the laughing stock of the industry."

"But why kidnap your own fake princess?"

"Jem, Jem, Jem," says Eric. "The Countess. I never could have fooled the Countess. My little Candy could easily fool you, but never real nobility."

You're absolutely furious, but you've got to remain in control. Count to ten.

. . . .

Now turn to page 36.

"You've got one minute to make up your mind and tell me about your secret power, Jem," Eric tells you. "Then, I turn you and the Princess over to Zipper."

If you're going to make a break for it, it's got to be soon. Eric may decide to tie you up, and without the use of your hands, you're helpless. You can't touch your Jemstar earrings and contact Synergy. It is now or never.

You desperately look around the room for an idea. You've got to create a diversion. The silence is broken only by the crackling sounds from the fireplace. A dying ember catches fire and sizzles, momentarily lighting the room. That's it!

Turn to page 19.

When you wake up, nothing seems very clear. Bit by bit, it all comes back. The knock-out gas, the plane taking off, Rio! You go over to the nearest window and look outside. Oh no!

"Rio," you shout, "Aja, Kimber, wake up, we're not in England, we're . . . I don't know *where* we are!"

Slowly Rio gets to his feet and looks out the window with you. He glances at his watch.

"We've been out for five hours," he tells you.

"We could be anywhere," Aja adds.

She's right—you could be anywhere. You see trees, water, palm trees. You're obviously someplace tropical. Off to the right, you spot a road which cuts through the jungle.

"Rio," you say, "there's a road which leads away from the plane. I think we should get off this plane while we can. Let's take that road."

"And go where?" asks Rio. "We have no supplies, no maps. We're safer if we stay here, until we can figure out where we are."

If you decide to wait on the plane, turn to page 30.
If you decide to take the road, turn to page 35.

"Yes, I think you're right, Jem," Aja tells you. "Let's go to the cellar first. But how do we get there?"

"I don't know," you say, "but maybe there's a door under the staircase. Follow me."

You hold the candle in front of you and in a short time find the door you're looking for.

"This must be it," you say, opening the door.

"It's awfully dark inside," Aja says, peering through the door.

You step through and Aja follows closely at your heels. Ouch! The two of you bump right into a wall.

Turn to page 22.

"Quiet, Jem," Aja says, standing up. "You'll wake the dead. I thought this was supposed to be a surprise party."

The three of you have a fit of giggling. Then you set off across the drawbridge. The castle actually has a moat!

"We can't just walk up to the front door and ring the bell," says Shana. "Who do we ask for, the kidnappers?"

"But that is just what we are going to do," you answer. "After we make a few changes."

You touch your Jemstar earrings, and instantly you, Aja, and Shana are transformed into three punk rockers, complete with spiked hairdos. When you ring the bell to the great hall of the castle, it's answered by someone you've met before. It's Zipper—a thug who works for your old enemy, Eric Raymond. Somehow you knew he was involved! Zipper stands in the doorway and gawks at you. He likes what he sees.

"Hello, Love," he says. "What can I do for you three ladies?"

"Our wheels broke down," Shana says. "Can you give us a hand?"

"My pleasure," he says. "Just lead the way." Shana and Zipper go off toward the car, and Zipper doesn't notice that you and Aja slip inside the door to the castle.

. . . .

Turn to page 41.

Immediately, bats fly out from the corners of the room and hover around Eric and the thug. They are so busy swiping at the bats that they don't see Aja coming from behind the barrels.

"Aiiee," she yells as she rushes out. She spin kicks the thug and karate chops Eric. They both fall to the ground unconscious.

"Good work," you tell her, as you untie Sarah.

"Am I glad to see you," Sarah says, laughing.

"Well," you tell her, "Eric is going to pay for this. As soon as you're ready, we're going to call Scotland Yard."

"No!" shouts Sarah. "No police! Don't call the police!"

What's going on here?

Turn to page 58.

"You're right. We should stay on the plane," you tell Rio. "Maybe we can find out where we are or what happened to Sarah. I'll search the front of the plane while you look around back here. If anybody hears anyone coming, sing out."

You reach the cockpit and find a few maps, some empty coffee cups, and a half-eaten apple. No pilot. No crew. No Sarah. The apple reminds you how hungry you are. Maybe the others are having better luck. As you turn to leave, you see men approaching the plane. You run to the back.

"Someone's coming!" you say. "I think it's the pilot."

"Back to where you were," says Rio. "Pretend you're still out. We'll see what they do."

You hear the pilot climbing into the cockpit. Then you hear the engines revving up. Oh no! The plane is starting to move down the runway.

"Rio, let's jump off now while we still have a chance," Kimber says.

"No," says Rio. "It's too late to jump. We'll have to stay put."

What do *you* say?

If you decide to stay on the plane, turn to page 52.
If you decide to jump off the plane, turn to page 68.

The note is typed. There are no clues as to who wrote it or what they want with you.

"Countess," you say, "do you know anything about the castle mentioned in the note?"

"I'm afraid I've never been there—although it is very close by," the Countess answers. "I can draw you a map showing you how to get there. The place is open to tourists during the summer. But now it should be closed."

"Well," you say, "someone is planning a special opening for me."

"You're not going!" says Shana, breathless. "It has to be a trap."

"Jem," says Kimber, "let us all go with you. We can surprise them and rescue the Princess. It's safer that way. I won't let you put yourself in danger."

"I don't know, Kimber," you say. "I think I might have to go alone. The Princess's life could be in danger. It would be safer for her if I follow their instructions."

. . . .

What should you do? If you decide to follow Kimber's advice and take the Holograms with you, turn to page 53.

If you decide to go alone, turn to page 42.

31

"Rio," you say. "We might as well get started. I have the feeling we're going to be doing a lot of walking."

You start walking along the edge of the runway to the road leading out of the airport.

"This would be a beautiful place to spend a vacation," Kimber says. "If only we knew where we were."

It *is* awfully hot. The road seems to be leading nowhere. Then, you hear a motor behind you.

"Jem, do you hear that?" Aja is practically shouting. "I think it's a car!" The car is a Jeep. As it gets closer, it slows down. You can see a policeman inside. He stops the Jeep and gets out. Great! You're saved. At last you've found help.

"Good day," he says. "May I see some identification, please?" He speaks English. What more could you hope for?

"Identification," you say. "Listen, we've been kidnapped, zapped with knock-out gas. We need help."

"You have no identification?" he asks.

"But, . . ." you try to say.

Turn to page 39.

"All right, Aja," you say, "I think you're right. We can't waste time exploring every room in this old castle. Let's go directly to the tower room."

You and Aja tiptoe past the open door and stop in front of the door leading to the tower room. You listen at the door, and hear faint voices inside.

"What are they saying?" Aja whispers.

"I can't tell. But one is a girl's voice."

You and Aja look around. You're standing in front of a solid wooden door. There is a window in the hallway to the right.

"Try the window," you tell Aja. "Can we get outside that way?"

Aja opens the window and leans out. "There's a narrow ledge out here," she says. "I think we might be able to use it to walk around and surprise whomever is inside the room."

"Maybe," you say, "but I think we should just knock on the door and see what happens."

. . . .

If you knock on the door, turn to page 44.
If you use the ledge, turn to page 48.

33

Holding the candle in front of you, you lead Aja toward the steps at the end of the corridor. Cobwebs cling to the walls and hang from the ceiling. You push them away from your face. Dustballs float up from the floor.

"Oh, no!" cries Aja, "Oh, no!"

"What? What is it?" you say, suddenly stopping.

"I think I'm m . . . I'm going to . . . sneeze . . ."

Turn to page 56.

"Perhaps you're right," Rio says. "Let's try the road."

You follow the road through the jungle. The sweet aroma of tropical flowers and spice plants fills the air. You hear cries of birds and wild animals.

"Have you any idea where we are?" you ask Rio.

"The Canary Islands maybe, or the Caribbean. Who knows?" he answers.

The road turns into a dirt path. You're getting tired and you're hungry.

"Do you think we can find something to eat?" Kimber asks.

"Sure," says Rio. "Stay here a minute and rest. I'll scout around."

Turn to page 50.

"*You're* behind all this trouble," says Rio.

"Quite right," says Eric, amused. "No hard feelings, I hope. My pilot got a little carried away with that knock-out gas."

"No hard feelings," says Rio, as he calmly steps forward and pushes Eric into the pool. When Zipper rushes forward, you neatly trip him. He goes flying into the pool as well.

"Outrageous!" shout Kimber and Aja.

"We have a great act," says Rio.

"Act," you say, getting an idea. "Aja, Kimber, we're going to give a special performance. Quick, into the cabana." You pull the rehearsal tape out of your pocket.

"Rio, put this tape on and announce our act in about fifteen minutes."

"Jem," says Aja, "we look awful. We have no costumes, no makeup, no music, no Shana."

"Stop complaining," you say. "We'll just improvise."

Zipper and Eric pull themselves out of the pool.

"You'll pay for this!" shouts Eric.

"No," you answer, "you'll pay!"

. . . .

Turn to page 72.

When you walk through the iron gate, you find yourself on a beautiful lawn. In the distance you can see a crystal blue pool. People are swimming, dancing and eating!

"Jem!" someone behind you shouts.

You stop in your tracks.

"Aren't you Jem, the rock star?" a young man asks, walking toward you.

"Yes," you say.

"Eric never mentioned you'd be here," he says.

Eric! Eric Raymond!

That snake! Have you walked right into his nest?

Turn to page 51.

"Eric," you say, stalling for time, "believe me when I tell you that there is no secret power. It's just your imagination."

Eric's fist slams down hard on the table. Zipper looks at you menacingly. You can hear the thunder outside. *Boom! Boom! Boom!* Or is that your heart beating?

"Don't try to bluff me, Jem," he yells.

"All right," you say. "You're too smart for me, Eric. You've won."

You look over at Sarah. You've got to come up with a story that Eric will believe so you can get Sarah out of here.

"This bracelet I'm wearing," you tell Eric. "It contains a minicomputer that does what I tell it to. This is my secret."

"You think I'm stupid?" shouts Eric. "You think I'll fall for such a silly story? Your power comes from your jewelry! That's a laugh!"

Turn to page 66.

"Well, you will have to come with me to headquarters. We have to be careful about smugglers on our lovely island."

"Don't you recognize us?" asks Kimber. "We're the Holograms and this is Jem, the famous rock star."

"Jem, so you're here to smuggle gems and your gang is called the Holograms," he says.

"No," you say, "wait, I can explain."

Too late. He escorts you into the Jeep. It looks like you're going to be explaining for a long time. Sarah has waited this long to be rescued; she's just going to have to wait a bit longer. Right now your adventure is at an

END.

"I hear guitar music!" you say.

"You're right, Jem," says Aja. "I hear it too!"

"Well, what are we sitting here for? Let's go investigate." At once, you start walking down the road. After a short time, the music becomes louder and louder. It seems to be coming from the west. You spot a footpath and show the others.

"This could be what we're looking for," says Rio.

Within minutes, you find yourself in front of a huge iron fence. The gates are locked but you can see a beautiful villa in the distance.

"What do you think, Jem?" asks Kimber. "Should we go inside?"

"I'm too tired to go on," you say. "Let's take a chance. At least we'll find out where we are."

Turn to page 37.

You and Aja enter the hallway. A candelabra lights the entrance way. Both of you take a lit candle and start to explore the nearest rooms. But first you call on Synergy to transform you back into your normal look.

"It's kind of spooky in here," whispers Aja, following closely on your heels.

"We'll stick close together," you say.

A sudden clanging noise scares both of you, and you bump into each other.

"What was that?" gasps Aja.

"I think it came from the cellar. Let's take a look," you say, turning around. Aja is gone!

"Aja? Aja? Where are you?" you whisper.

"Over here, Jem," says Aja. "And, be quiet." When you find her, Aja has started to climb a set of stairs that lead to the second floor.

"Jem," she says, "when we were walking across that bridge in front of the castle, I am sure I saw a light in the tower room. Just now I heard voices—one was a woman's voice. It could be Sarah."

"Aja," you say, "didn't you hear that clang? It came from the cellar. Maybe we should look downstairs first."

. . . .

Where do you want to search for Sarah?
The tower room? Turn to page 11.
The cellar? Turn to page 27.

41

"I'm going to follow the instructions in the note and go alone," you say. "Try not to worry. If I'm not back in two hours, call Rio. Then call Scotland Yard."

"Be careful, Jem!" says Aja. "Are you *sure* you don't want me to come with you? I'd like the chance to use some of my karate on those cowards."

You shake your head "no" and say goodbye. You take a flashlight and the map drawn by the Countess. A half hour later, you reach the drawbridge leading to Tannington Castle. You park the car and walk across. The only sound you hear is your footsteps on the stone walkway. Eventually, you find yourself in front of what once was the entrance to the great hall.

"A full moon," you say aloud. "As if things weren't weird enough." Then, suddenly, there's a flash of lightning. Dark clouds roll across the moon, and thunder booms in the distance. "Okay, Jem, no more stalling," you tell yourself. This is not Transylvania and Dracula is not waiting for you inside. Nothing's going to happen. "You're not afraid," you tell yourself. You try the door. It's unlocked. Slowly you enter the hall. No one home. Maybe you should leave.

"Hello, Love!" a voice from inside says. Why does that voice sound so familiar?

. . . .

Turn to page 21.

You and Aja step into a tiny room no bigger than a closet. You listen as the footsteps come nearer. Then, you hear metal on metal. Someone is locking the door to the room you're hiding in!

"Did you put the bags in the car?" the voice outside the door says. You recognize it. It's Pizzazz! The Misfits are here.

"Yes," replies Stormer.

"Okay, then," Pizzazz replies, "we're out of here! We have a plane to catch. Everything here is locked up tight."

That includes you and Aja. But you've gotten out of tight spots before. You'll think of something—won't you?

THE END

"We'll try the door," you say. "Just let me listen, again." As you place your ear to the door, you hear someone shout, "Untie me NOW!"

You've got to act fast. It sounds like something is going to happen inside the room. "Aja," you say, "get ready. I'll knock on the door. When someone answers, I'll step aside and you knock them down."

"Ready!" says Aja as she gets into her karate stance.

You pound on the door and quickly step aside. The door opens a tiny bit. Aja rushes the door and jumps inside.

"Aiiee," she shouts. Then there is silence. Finally Aja calls, "Jem, come quick."

Oh, no! You fear the worst. Are you too late? Did you make a mistake? You rush into the room. You're shocked!

"What took you so long?" says Sarah, as you enter the room.

Sarah has Eric Raymond neatly tied to a chair and is playing checkers with him.

"Let's go!" says Sarah. "No, wait," she adds, "he owes me $10. He may be a king rat—but your Mr. Raymond isn't much at checkers!"

THE END

This kind-looking woman is related to that snake. You instinctively take a step back.

The old woman walks around the room lighting more candles. You and Aja sit on an old divan covered with a white sheet.

"Eric is always getting himself into trouble," she says. "I'm afraid he's gone too far this time! I saw him bring that young girl into my house. He and that awful Zipper person are up to no good."

She leans close to you and Aja and whispers, "If I tell you where to find her, will you give me your word you won't turn my grandson in to the police?"

You and Aja look at each other. The old woman reminds you of someone but you can't quite remember who. It's on the tip of your tongue. Who is she? Can you trust her?

Turn to page 15.

"I think we should follow the Mercedes's tire tracks before it gets too far ahead," you say.

"That's a good idea, Jem," says Kimber, opening the trunk of the car and taking out a jack. "It's a good thing I took that auto mechanics class in high school."

Within ten minutes the girls have changed the tire. You drive in the direction the Mercedes went. Soon you notice that the road ends and the tracks lead off the road across a field.

The field is muddy and full of rocks. You don't know if the spare tire will make it on this kind of terrain. You'd better follow the tracks on foot.

"Listen, Shana," you say, "take the car and go back to the Countess's estate. Call Rio and tell him what happened. Kimber, Aja, and I will track the Mercedes on foot. It can't have gotten too far ahead on this road."

"Okay, but be careful, Jem," says Shana. "It'll be dark soon."

Turn to page 16.

"I don't like this," says Kimber, stepping into the plane. "It could be trouble."

Just as the three of you get inside, you see a Jeep driving up to the plane. Who could it be?

"Quick, hide behind these seats," you whisper. You hold your breath.

The Jeep stops. Someone is coming into the plane, but you can't see who it is from your hiding place. The sound of footsteps echoes on the metal ladder. Then silence.

"Okay, girls," a voice says. "I know you're here. Come out."

You know that voice!

Turn to page 5.

"You're right," you tell Aja. "I think we should try the ledge. Then at least we'll have the element of surprise on our side."

You and Aja step cautiously out of the window. Once on the ledge, you begin to wonder if you've made a mistake. With your faces to the wall, you edge your way around the tower.

"Careful," you tell Aja. "If we fall, we go into the moat."

When you reach the other side of the tower, you find yourself in front of a six-paned window.

"Will it open?" asks Aja.

"I'm not sure. Give it a try."

Aja puts both hands on the sill and pushes. Nothing, at first. Then, it moves. No, it doesn't move. You moved! What! The ledge—it's crumbling! You're falling. You hold your nose and take a dive into the moat.

This rescue idea was all wet—and you've left Princess Sarah high and dry!

THE END

As you and Sarah cross the drawbridge, she asks you, "What do you think made the fireplace explode, Jem?"

"I can't imagine," you reply. "You can never tell what will happen in these old castles. But, it certainly was our good fortune."

You're a little breathless as you and Sarah finally reach the car. Sarah gets there first. She opens the door, then straightens up and stands perfectly still.

"Jem," she says, "we're not quite home free!"

You look into the car. Zipper is sitting in the passenger seat holding your keys!

"Hello, Love," he says. "I don't think you're going anywhere without these."

He's right. This adventure is stalled, stopped, and out of gas.

THE END

Within minutes Rio returns with mangoes and papayas. He neatly pares and slices the fruit with his pocket knife. You have never tasted anything so wonderful in your whole life.

The sounds of the jungle are like music. How beautiful, you think. Without realizing it, you start to hum along.

Suddenly you sit up straight.

"Rio, do you hear music?" you ask.

"Yes," he says, "it's just the sound of the jungle."

"You think so? Since when do animals play guitars?" you ask.

"Guitars!" say Aja and Kimber in unison.

. . . .

Turn to page 40.

"Eric!" you say. "Eric Raymond! Is *he* here?"

"Why, yes," continues the young man. "What a wonderful surprise. Jem, here, in person. Could I possibly persuade you to sing?"

"Maybe later," answers Rio. He takes you by the arm and steers you away. You look over your shoulder and see Kimber and Aja heading for the food.

"Don't look now," says Rio, "but our royal Princess is sitting over there, and she doesn't look very uncomfortable."

"What?" you say. "Are you suggesting she's a guest?"

Suddenly a loud shrill scream fills the air, followed by a splash. Turning around, you see Pizzazz emerging from the pool.

"Rio," you say, "I am beginning to smell a rat."

"Speaking of rats," says Rio, "here comes Eric Raymond."

Sure enough, Raymond is slowly walking toward you. "Jem, my dear. How nice of you to drop in," he says through his gritted teeth.

. . . .

Turn to page 8.

"You're right, Rio," you say. "It's too late to jump. We'll just have to stay on the plane and see where we go."

"Well, we might at least enjoy the ride. I found some chocolate bars in the back," says Kimber, passing out the candy.

"Everyone find a seat and buckle up," says Rio. "If the pilot hears us back here, we may get a second blast of that knock-out gas."

"Don't worry about that," you say. "When I was searching the cockpit, I saw the fuel tanks and the dial registered near empty. We're not going very far."

As if on cue, the plane starts to take a nose dive and spin crazily.

"Whattt'sss happenningg?" you try to say, as you stumble around.

"I'm going to try to reach the cockpit," says Rio, undoing his seat belt.

"I'm going with you," you say, hanging onto the seat in front.

You and Rio are tossed from side to side. Moving forward is like heading into a wind tunnel. It seems to take hours to move just a few inches. At last, you reach the pilot's cabin. As you look inside, you feel as if someone has just punched you in the stomach.

Turn to page 57.

Kimber's right, you decide. With the Holograms' help you may be able to sneak up on the kidnappers and surprise them.

"I think you may be right," you say. "In fact, I already have a plan."

"Kimber," you say, "you should stay here in case the kidnappers try to reach us. If you don't hear from me in two hours, call Rio and tell him what happened."

You want to be sure Kimber is in a safe place. After all, she is your sister. You'd never forgive yourself if she got hurt. You can tell Kimber is disappointed, but she knows better than to argue with you about something like this.

"Aja, Shana, this may be dangerous. Are you sure you want to come along?"

"Yes," they reply. "Let's do it!"

"Good," you think to yourself. Aja's karate could come in handy, and Shana is good at staying cool under pressure.

Turn to page 67.

As you start to leave, you hear a commotion in the hallway and go to investigate. The security guard is escorting two young women to the elevator. It's Pizzazz and Stormer—members of the Misfits, the rock group that *lives* to make trouble for you and the Holograms.

"Take your grubby paws off me," Pizzazz tells the guard. "You'll contaminate my outfit."

"Outfit," says the guard. "You'll go 'out' on the end of my foot! Take your snooping elsewhere, my girls!"

What are Pizzazz and Stormer doing in London? How long were they eavesdropping—and what trouble are they planning?

Should you follow the Misfits and try to find out where they are going?

Or should you forget them, and drive to the Countess's estate with the Princess?

. . . .

If you follow the Misfits, turn to page 9.
If you drive to the Countess's estate, turn to page 61.

54

As the old woman runs across the room, she looks down at the floor.

"Snakes," she yells, "I hate snakes!"

She jumps up on the chair and the sudden movement makes her wig fall off. You recognize her at once. It's Pizzazz!

"Aja, Shana," you yell, "don't let her escape! It's Pizzazz. We've been tricked!"

Shana neatly pulls her down from the chair and Aja sits on top of her.

"Get off me," Pizzazz yells. "You'll flatten me like a pancake."

"Be quiet, Pizzazz," you say, "or we'll use you for a trampoline. Now, tell us: where is Eric holding the Princess?"

"Don't hold your breath waiting for *me* to tell you," sneers Pizzazz. "Or, better yet, hold your breath. And, take a hike while you're at it."

"She'll never talk," says Aja. "Let me use my 'hairdo hold' on her."

"Oh, no!" you say, winking at Aja. "Isn't that the one in which the girl had her hair torn out at the roots?"

Pizzazz appears to be falling for this bluff. You try to keep yourself from laughing.

"I'll talk! I'll talk!" cries Pizzazz.

. . . .

Turn to page 13.

"Ah, ah, ah, choo! Ah, choo!" Aja sneezes.

The candle flickers. You cup your hand around the flame. Somehow it doesn't go out!

"Shush," you whisper to Aja, who holds her finger under her nose.

"I'm all right, now," she says.

You and Aja continue down the corridor. Finally, you reach the steps.

"We made it," Aja says, still holding her nose.

The two of you climb the steps. They narrow, then twist. It seems as if you're climbing forever.

"I don't like this," you tell Aja. "There's something wrong."

There's something wrong, all right. When you reach the top of the steps, there's no rope and no doorway.

. . . .

Turn to page 17.

The pilot's cabin is empty! He has bailed out and left you and your friends alone!! You look around the cabin in desperation. You see a bin marked *parachutes*. Bracing yourself to keep from falling, you open the box. Someone has slashed the silk of the chutes! You sink into the copilot's seat and look over at Rio.

"I'm sorry, Rio," you say. "I got you into this mess, but, we'll figure a way out, somehow."

Aja and Kimber appear at the cabin door. They quickly realize the situation.

"Jem," gasps Kimber, "do something!"

"Don't panic," you say. "Go back and buckle yourselves into the seats. We may crash so brace yourselves."

You glance over at Rio who's taken over the controls.

"You can fly this plane!?" you ask incredulously.

"Yes," he says coolly, "I could—if we had a map, if we had enough gas, and if we could find a landing strip!"

Turn to page 62.

"Sarah," you say, "what's wrong?"

"Oh, dear," she answers. "Eric somehow got his hands on some silly letters I wrote. They're really quite harmless, but if he were to publish them it could embarrass my family."

"What kind of letters?" you ask.

"Well," she says, "they're love letters! And you know, a royal princess isn't like a regular teenage girl. We're supposed to be perfect."

"Sarah, do you know where Eric put the letters?" you ask, suddenly getting an idea.

"Yes!" Sarah says excitedly. "I remember now. I saw him hide them in a hidden compartment in the fireplace. I think I know the way to open it."

. . . .

Turn to page 69.

"We'll go right," you say, a little unsure of yourself.

You and Aja walk down the corridor. "Stop a minute," you tell Aja. "I think I hear footsteps."

You hold your breath and listen. "Yes," you whisper, "hurry, we have to find a place to hide."

You rush forward. Nothing. The corridor is leading nowhere, and there's no place to hide. Whoever is behind you is getting closer and closer.

"Here," you say, relieved. "We can hide in here!"

Turn to page 43.

In the distance you can hear a faint voice, a familiar voice.

"Goodbye, Jem," it says. "Sweet dreams."

You recognize the voice. It's Pizzazz. She was the old lady! Oh, no. How could you have been so trusting!

Don't look now, Jem. It looks like you're about to make your biggest hit.

THE END

You meet the Princess and the Holograms and head out for the Countess's estate. As you drive, you try to forget about Pizzazz and Stormer.

"Jem," Sarah says, "I know this may sound funny, but I think we're being followed."

Suddenly, you hear a loud noise and your car swerves all over the road. You struggle to control it. You're going to crash! Oh no! You hold tight to the steering wheel as the car speeds through some bushes near the edge of the road. You are thrown forward as it comes to a sudden stop.

Slowly, you, the Holograms, and Princess Sarah get out of the car. You're a little shaken.

"Is everyone all right?" you ask. "Anyone hurt?"

Everyone seems to be fine.

"What happened?" Kimber asks.

"We had a blowout," you tell them, when Aja interrupts you.

"Look!" Aja cries, "someone put nails on the pavement. This was no accident."

You hear a roaring noise coming down the road.

"What's that sound?" asks Shana.

You turn your head to look. What on earth??!!

Turn to page 23.

Rio taps his finger against the glass dial on the panel.

"Empty," he says. "Look out the window, Jem. No flat land. We can't land in the trees."

You desperately search the landscape for open space. "Maybe the dial is broken," you say hopefully. "We could have a full tank."

Almost immediately, the right engine starts to sputter. The propellers slow, then stop. Then the left engine sputters, but miraculously it starts running again. But for how long?

"Hang on," says Rio. "Brace yourself. We're going to make a crash landing."

You look over at Rio. You'd love to tell him your secret—that you're both Jerrica and Jem. All you have to do is touch your earrings, and he'll know. But . . .

Not just yet, you think. Let me look one more time. There *has* to be a place to land this plane!

Turn to page 14.

Rio advances toward Eric and pushes him hard—right into the pool. Eric comes up yelling and cursing—but the music is too loud, so the guests think he's just partying a little harder than usual!

Before you know it, one of the guests pushes another guest into the pool and then someone else picks up the idea. Before long, half the guests are in the pool laughing and splashing, and the other half are throwing things and screaming "Party! Party!" at the top of their lungs.

Don't look now, Jem, but this party has turned into a brawl. You'll have to wait for another time to get the solution to THE VIDEO CAPER mystery. But right now it looks like you're going for a swim.

SPLASH!

THE END

"Wait," you say to Aja. You whisper, "Something about that old woman is familiar but I just can't put my finger on it." You sense trouble.

"Mrs. Raymond," you turn to say, "could you get us another candle? It's awfully dark in there."

"Yes, my dear," she replies and walks over to the desk.

"Aja," you say quietly, "I think we should take the old lady with us and get her to take us to Eric. We can exchange her for Sarah."

"Okay, Jem," says Aja, "when she comes over here, I'll grab her."

The old lady walks toward you. When she hands you the candle, Aja grabs her arm. Suddenly you hear someone outside the room.

Whoever is outside the room is about to come in! Your heart beats faster as you see the doorknob turn.

Turn to page 12.

64

"Wait," says Kimber. "If anyone is around, they'll surely recognize you. Let me go."

"No, it's too dangerous," you say. You touch your Jemstar earrings and instantly transform yourself into Jerrica.

"Everyone may know me as Jem," you say, "but few people will recognize Jerrica."

You set out for the ticket shack. When you reach it, you knock loudly.

"Come on in. Door's open," a voice says.

"Hello," you say, entering. "I want to charter that airplane outside. Can you tell me where the pilot is?"

"Not for hire, lady," the clerk tells you. "That's a private plane. Belongs to an American gentleman. I just fueled it up. Says he's leaving soon."

"Thank you," you say. "I'll try somewhere else."

You leave quickly. You touch your earrings and transform back to Jem. Since Jerrica is supposed to be back in New York, it would be too risky to keep that identity for too long.

When you get back to Aja and Kimber, you tell them that the plane is fueled up and ready to take off. "We need to get inside for a better look before the pilot returns. Maybe Sarah is inside. Let's go."

Turn to page 47.

"I'll show you how the bracelet works," you say, stepping forward. "Just touch it and whisper what you want."

You slowly place the bracelet on the table. In spite of himself, Eric is beginning to believe you. He is distracted by the bracelet, so he doesn't see you touch your Jemstar earrings.

"Okay, Synergy," you whisper. "Do your thing!" An extremely bright white light fills the room, blinding Eric and Zipper. You quickly untie Sarah and race for the hallway. Before you leave, you pull the cord to the lamp, and the room is totally dark.

"How did you do that?" asks Sarah, as you race out of the castle and into your car.

"Do what?" you ask, all innocence.

"You know, the light—how did you do it?" Sarah persists.

"Oh, I didn't do anything. It was just lightning!"

Good line, Jem. It *was* lightning—your lightning-fast thinking and a little help from your secret friend, Synergy. Outrageous!

THE END

You, Aja, and Shana drive to the castle following the map drawn by the Countess. As you approach the front entrance, you turn off your lights.

"We'll park the car here," you say. "Aja, open the hood and pull out some part so the car will look disabled."

Aja quickly lifts the hood. "I wish I knew more about cars. Here goes nothing."

Aja falls to the ground after a loud pop. Sparks fly out from the car.

"Aja, Aja, are you okay? Are you hurt?" you yell.

Turn to page 28.

"I think you're right, Kimber. We should try to get off the plane now," you say.

As the plane taxis down the runway, it slows for a turn. Now is your best chance to jump out. Rio moves to the hatchway and slides the door open. The ground seems to be moving awfully fast!

"Jem, Kimber, Aja," says Rio. "Jump, now! Try to roll once you hit the ground. Quickly, before the pilot starts to speed up."

You hold your breath, cross your fingers and jump. Somehow you make it without breaking every bone in your body. Aja, Kimber, and Rio follow. All four of you run for cover in the trees. The pilot takes off almost immediately.

You watch the plane ascend and eventually disappear. Now what? The silence is unbearable. You don't know where you are. You don't know where you're going.

It's hot. You are standing on the edge of a runway in a clearing in a tropical jungle. A breeze and the smell of salt water tells you that you must be near the sea. Maybe you're on an island.

Turn to page 32.

You, Aja, and Sarah rush upstairs. Sarah shows you a room with the fireplace where Eric hid the letters.

"There's a little lever here someplace," she tells you, as she looks around the fireplace.

"Hurry, Sarah," you say. "Eric and that animal could wake up. And we've got to meet Shana back at the car or she'll come looking for us."

Suddenly, Sarah finds the lever and pulls it. A little drawer pops open. Inside is a small packet of letters tied with a pink ribbon. You light the fire and Sarah gleefully throws them in.

You are about to telephone Scotland Yard when the room starts to shake. Objects on the mantel rattle, and an unmistakable whirring sound fills the room.

"Outside," you yell. As you run out the door, you meet Shana coming in. But before she can say anything, you are practically blinded by a bright white light. You hear someone laughing. It's Eric. He's got Zipper and the other goon with him. You watch helplessly as they escape in a helicopter.

"Next time, Eric," you shout. "Next time!"

"Don't worry," Shana says putting an arm around your shoulder, "we did what we came to do—Sarah is safe."

"There's only one more thing we've got to do," Sarah says. "Celebrate!"

And that's just what you do, for the next six nights. Being in London with the Princess is a royal blast!

THE END

"Come on, Jem," Aja calls to you. "I'm sure we can trust the old lady. She's had every chance to call Eric if she wanted to."

You peer into the darkened passageway. You enter cautiously, holding your breath. So far, so good! Looks all right. You step back into the room and take a candle from the old woman.

"Go to the end of the passage," she tells you. "Then, climb the steps. At the top of the steps you'll see a door with a rope. Pull the rope. It opens the secret door in the tower room."

"Right," you say. "Let's go!"

You and Aja start down the secret passageway. "Yuck!" says Aja, "I don't think I'm going to like this place."

Turn to page 34.

"Left," you say.

Sticking close together, you and Aja follow the hallway until you come to what looks like an old wine cellar.

"Look at all those old wine barrels," says Aja. "I just had an awful thought. Do you think Sarah could be in one of them?"

"Shush," you whisper. "I heard voices from over there." You and Aja edge closer to the barrels and listen.

"We'll fix it so this kidnapping looks as if Jem and her boyfriend were behind it," says a voice. "It'll ruin that new video of hers. The Misfits will step in and be bigger than ever."

"That voice," you whisper, "is *too* familiar. Let's try to get a look at who's talking."

You and Aja peek out from behind a barrel. Two men sit at a table; both have their backs to you. You can't quite see their faces but you can see Sarah. She is tied to a chair, facing you.

Suddenly one of the men says, "Boss, I think I heard a noise behind those barrels."

You've got to do something!

Turn to page 18.

You, Aja, and Kimber enter the cabana. You shower and change.

"Okay, Synergy," you say, touching your Jemstar earrings, "Showtime."

When you and the Holograms come out of the cabana, you look outrageous. Your concert costumes glitter in the sun, and the music begins. Rio announces you and you step up to the microphone.

"Ladies and gentlemen," you say, "we are pleased to entertain you today with a benefit concert."

You look over at Eric to be sure he is listening.

"Eric Raymond has generously agreed to double our fee and donate it to our special charity—Starlight House for Girls."

Applause!

"And, he has agreed to match any donation you may wish to make."

"Now," you add, "Showtime! Let's rock 'n' roll."

THE END